D0523200

Elmo's
ABC
Book

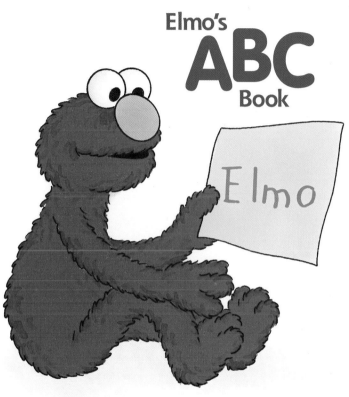

Elmo

By Sarah Albee
Illustrated by Tom Brannon

Dalmatian Press, LLC, 2005. All rights reserved.
Published by Dalmatian Press, LLC, 2005. The DALMATIAN PRESS name and logo are trademarks of Dalmatian Press, LLC, Franklin, Tennessee 37067. No part of this book may be reproduced or copied in any form without written permission from the copyright owner.

Printed in the U.S.A.
ISBN: 1-40371-043-0 (X) 1-40371-351-0 (M)

05 06 07 08 LBM 10 9 8 7 6 5 4 3 2 1
13804 Sesame Street 8x8 Storybook: Elmo's ABC Book

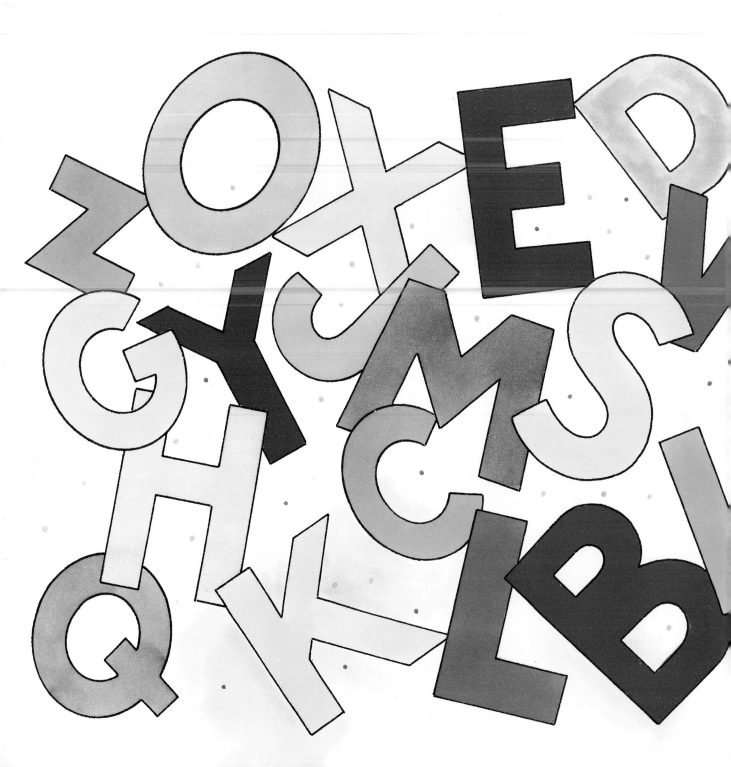

Hello! Elmo is trying to decide
what Elmo's favorite letter is.
Will you help Elmo?

Oh, thank you!

Elmo loves apples
because they are delicious and crunchy.
And apples start with the letter A.
So A must be Elmo's favorite letter.

But wait! Baby starts with the letter B.
And Elmo loves babies, too. So B must be
Elmo's favorite letter. Right, baby?

Crayon and cat begin with the letter C.
So Elmo thinks that maybe C is Elmo's
favorite letter.

Oh, but Elmo LOVES dogs! Hello, doggies!
And doggie starts with the letter D.

Uh, oh! Elmo just remembered that
Elmo's name begins with the letter E.

But Elmo's fur is very fuzzy and fluffy.
So F must be Elmo's favorite letter!

But green grapes make a great snack.

And grapes begin with the letter G!

Coming home for a hug
is one of Elmo's favorite things.
So H must be the one.
Ha ha ha! Tee hee hee!

Oh, but Elmo loves
to use Elmo's imagination!
And I is the first letter
in imagination!

Could it be **J**? Elmo is a very good joke teller.
Would you like to hear Elmo's joke?

Knock, knock.
Who's there?
Boo.
Boo who?
Please don't cry.

Elmo just realized
that kangaroo starts
with the letter K.

How do you do,
little kangaroo?

Oh, but L is the first letter in the word love.
Elmo just *loves* love!

Monster starts with M.

Elmo is a little monster and so are Elmo's friends.

So M must be Elmo's favorite letter.

Elmo can make a lot of noisy noise! Wheeee!!!

And so can an octopus.

Do you think N or O could be Elmo's favorite letter?

P is the first letter in the word poem.
And Elmo just wrote this poem called
"Q is for Quilt."
Is Q Elmo's favorite letter?

Q is for quilt.
It's cozy on my bed.
It keeps me
warm and snuggly
From my toes
up to my head.

by
Elmo

Elmo also loves riddles:

What did the sea say to the sand?
Nothing. It just waved.

R must be Elmo's favorite letter!

Can Elmo tell you a secret?

Elmo thinks that you have a very nice smile.

So maybe S is Elmo's favorite letter.

Turtles are terrific! And guess what?
Turtle begins with a T.

Toodle-oo, turtle!

Toodle-oo!

Ha ha ha! Hee hee hee! Elmo is upside-down.

And Elmo likes to listen to the violin! So is Elmo's favorite letter U? Or is it V?

Elmo wishes he could decide which is his
favorite letter. What about W? Or X?
Could it be Y?
Why, oh why, can't Elmo decide!